THE SECRETS OF DROON

The Chariot
of Queen Zara

by Tony Abbott
Illustrated by David Merrell
Cover illustration by Tim Jessell

A
LITTLE APPLE
PAPERBACK

SCHOLASTIC INC.
New York Toronto London Auckland Sydney
Mexico City New Delhi Hong Kong Buenos Aires

For Janie and Lucy,
my two queens of light

For more information about the continuing saga of Droon,
please visit Tony Abbott's website at
www.tonyabbottbooks.com

ISBN 0-439-67175-2

12 11 10 9 8 7 6 5 4 3 2   6 7 8 9 10 11/0

Printed in the U.S.A.   40
First printing, April 2006

Contents

One

Over the Volcano

Eric Hinkle looked down into the fiery volcano and knew he was falling too fast.

"We're supposed to be flying," he said. "You said you would fly us down here."

"I know that," said his friend Julie Rubin, clutching him tightly by the hand and trying to slow down.

"But we're not flying," yelled Eric, starting to feel the volcano's heat. "We're *falling*!"

"I know that, too!" said Julie.

Eric and Julie, along with their friends Neal Kroger; Princess Keeah; King Zello; Queen Relna; Khan, the king of the Lumpies; and Max, the spider troll, had just jumped through an opening in Calibaz, the strange shadowland next to Eric's town in the Upper World. They were descending into the magical world of Droon, where Julie had agreed to fly them.

"Are we going to crash?" cried Khan, holding on to Relna and Keeah for dear life. "Because it feels like we're going to crash!"

"Not if I can help it!" said Max, busily spinning a web of spider silk.

Eric really hoped they wouldn't crash.

Just minutes before, he had found the mysterious Pearl Sea, a part of Queen Zara's awesome Moon Medallion. From the Pearl Sea they had learned that their long-lost wizard friend Galen was trapped on the far side of Droon's moon.

Eric and his friends were all determined to rescue the great wizard.

If only they survived their fall.

"Are you even *trying* to slow down?" asked Neal.

"I am!" said Julie, struggling. "But I've never flown so many people before!"

"We're in the Dark Lands," said Relna. "Remember that your powers may turn against you. Maybe we can help. Keeah—"

Together, Relna and her daughter aimed their fingertips at the ground, showering the air with sparks in an effort to slow their fall.

Right, thought Eric as they began to tumble even faster. *There's the whole power thing.*

Since he, Julie, and Neal had found a magic staircase in Eric's basement that led them to Droon, powers had come to them, too. For instance, Julie had gained the ability to fly, which she was usually really good at. And even though Neal didn't seem to have any powers, he had been transformed into several different creatures, including a bug and a goblin.

Best of all, Eric himself was becoming a major wizard. He could shoot silver sparks from his fingertips. He had visions of the future, and he could read weird old languages without even trying. He even suspected that the strange Sword of Zara he found in Calibaz was magically keeping him safe.

But the oddest thing was finding the mysterious and wonderful Pearl Sea in his house. His own house!

Eric couldn't understand that at all.

In fact, he hardly understood any of it.

Why me? he thought. *I mean, really! Why me?*

But looking down, he realized he never *would* understand, unless they slowed down very soon.

"Eric, we need your help!" cried Keeah, her long blond hair flying across her face. "Blast the air. Try to slow our fall —"

But when he added his own sparks to hers, the friends only seemed to fall faster.

"Noooooo!" he screamed.

All of a sudden — *flooop!* — a vast wispy canopy of spider silk billowed above them, slowing them immediately. In an instant, the eight friends were drifting gently to the ground.

"So much for wizard tricks!" said Max. "Good old spider silk comes to the rescue!"

"Thank you, Max," said King Zello as they floated softly to the base of the great volcano.

The children shivered to remember the

first time they had seen the eerie black mountain called Kano. It had long been the palace of the once very powerful — and very evil — sorcerer known as Lord Sparr.

Recently, however, Sparr had been transformed into a boy, and he was helping the kids battle two even worse enemies — Emperor Ko, ruler of the beasts, and the wicked moon dragon Gethwing. In fact, Sparr was with the beasts right then, secretly hoping to defeat their armies from within.

Like the sorcerer's other former lairs left behind when he became young, the volcano palace lay deep in Droon's Dark Lands, surrounded by thousands of square miles of black earth, charred trees, smoky air, and evil.

"The Dark Lands always remind me of Calibaz and the hoobahs who live there," said Neal, gazing back up toward the cloudy world they had just come from.

Everyone remembered the froglike hoobahs. A legend said that they were doomed to wander the shadowland until a hero led them into the light. "Someday," Neal added, "their dream will come true."

"Yes, and *our* dream to find Galen can only come true if we hide," said Max, pointing with one of his eight legs. "Look who's coming!"

Eeee! Eeee! Three snakelike beasts with wings of fire soared over the distant black hills and swooped quickly toward them.

"Wingsnakes," said Relna. "Probably spies for Emperor Ko. Everyone, hide. In the volcano!"

"*In* the volcano?" said Neal. "Oh, man!"

The eight friends scrambled over broken rocks to an entrance at the base of the fiery mountain. They dived in just before the wingsnakes were close enough to see them.

The walls inside the volcano were charred black. Plumes of smoke rose into clouds that were lit with flickering flames and the glow of molten lava. Beyond the smoke, the children could make out ominous dark passages twisting deep into the mountain.

"Very nice place," grumbled Khan.

Kano had always been home to the Ninns, Sparr's former army of large red warriors. But looking around, the friends saw bent and broken Ninn weapons strewn across the volcano floor, along with cracked pots and the remains of hastily abandoned cooking fires.

Zello shared a look with Relna. "Perhaps the Ninns were forced to leave. Maybe the beasts took over and live here now."

Eeee! Eeee! The wingsnakes called to one another, circling the volcano.

Neal groaned as they all moved away

from the entrance. "I knew this was a bad idea. We're trapped in here."

"Trapped, but not caught yet," said Julie.

Khan frowned suddenly. "Don't speak too soon," he whispered. "Look there —"

As an odd-shaped shadow slid along the wall, they realized that something else was inside the volcano, moving in one of the passages. Lit from behind by the flames, the thing — whatever it was — drew closer, and its shadow grew larger until it dwarfed the friends.

King Zello raised his club. Eric drew the Sword of Zara from his belt and held it aloft.

"Point your fingers, Mom," said Keeah as she and Relna aimed at the silhouette of a big head moving across the wall.

"Please make it go away," whispered Neal.

A second head moved next to the first.

"Please make *them* go away!" said Neal.

"Maybe there are a hundred of them!" cried Julie.

Eric's sword quivered in his hands. "All in all," he said, "I think I'd rather be falling —"

Then came an inhuman wail and a sudden rush of feet, and the beasts charged into the cave.

Two

A Fruit by Any Other Name

"Ahh!" Max screamed. *"Ahhhhh!"*

Then he stopped. "Wait. What?"

There weren't a hundred beasts. There weren't even two beasts. There was only one. It had two cute heads, was small and furry, drooled a lot, and they had seen it before.

"It's Kem!" said Eric, lowering his sword. "It's Sparr's little puppy!"

"Come here, boy!" called Neal. He bent down, and the dog ran right into his arms.

"Are you lost, Kem? Huh?" said Neal. "Are you looking for your master?"

Kem had been a wild, vicious, adult dog before he, too, had been transformed along with Sparr and had become a puppy.

"Sorry, boy," said Julie. "But Sparr's not here."

At the mention of his master's name, Kem howled — *"Roooo!"* — leaped out of Neal's arms, and scampered away. He returned in a flash, rolling a fruit the size of a coconut across the volcano floor.

Keeah blinked. "Is that what I think it is?"

"It's a tangfruit," said her mother.

Everyone backed away from the dog. They all knew what a tangfruit was. If you removed its hard shell, it smelled like a combination of garbage and an old moldy cellar. Tangfruit smelled rotten. It smelled *worse* than rotten.

But tangfruit wasn't all bad. As foul as its smell was, its flavor was actually sweet. And anyone who ate it could understand the speech of animals.

"*Rrrrr,*" Kem snuffled, pushing the tangfruit around with his paws.

"Wait," said Eric suddenly. "What if he's not *looking* for Sparr? What if . . . Kem, do you have a *message* from Sparr?"

"*Roooo!*" Kem howled expectantly.

"I think he wants one of us to eat it," said Zello, taking a further step back.

"Of course, I can't," said Khan, joining the king. "Not with my sensitive nose."

"I vote for Neal," said Julie. "He loves to eat."

"Yes," said Relna. "Neal, you eat it."

Neal gave his friends a look. "Yeah, I don't think so. Why me?"

"Kem likes you, don't you, boy?" said Max.

The puppy appeared to nod. "*Roo-ooo!*"

"Uh-huh, and I like Kem," said Neal. "But I haven't had lunch yet. And if I spoil my appetite, my mom gets really mad. Besides, although it doesn't always seem like it, I eat food. Tangfruit is not food. It's . . . it's . . ."

Kem leaped back into Neal's arms and licked him with both tongues. "*Rooo?*"

"Oh, man! Are you serious?" said Neal. "Unbelievable. What I do for Droon! Okay, someone crack it open while I hold my nose —"

Heaving his club, Zello smashed the fruit's shell, and a terrible smell filled the cave.

"Oh, not a good moment for me!" Khan sniffed, swallowing a big breath and holding it.

Picking up a piece of the fruit, Neal pushed it into his mouth. "Uck, uck . . . oh . . . whoa!" He smiled suddenly and licked his lips and fingers. "This is good. This is *really* good!"

As Neal gobbled it up, and the smell finally faded, Kem snuffled and grunted softly. After about five minutes, the dog finally went quiet.

"Wow, that's some story!" said Neal.

"Tell us," said Queen Relna.

"Okay," said Neal. "Sparr was able to stop in Kano for only a couple of minutes before Gethwing flew him away. But he told Kem three things while he was here. First, Emperor Ko is planning something really big in the Serpent Sea, involving a lot of sea beasts —"

"Oh, this is not good," said King Zello, pacing back and forth and slapping his giant club into his palm. "No, not good at all."

"What's the second thing?" asked Julie.

"Sparr's not quite sure," said Neal, "but he thinks that Agrah-Voor is in trouble, and it has something to do with Ko's big plans."

The kids remembered their brief time in Agrah-Voor. That haven of Droon's slain heroes was known as "the land of the lost." Those who had died fighting against evil in Droon waited in Agrah-Voor for the day when they could return to a world at peace.

"And the third thing?" asked Queen Relna.

Neal bent to the dog. "Did you say what I think you said?" Kem's heads murmured in unison. Neal sighed. "You *did* say that."

"What is it?" asked Keeah. "What did Kem say? Something about Galen?"

Neal nodded. "Kem said that there is a

secret hidden in Sparr's old castle at Plud. Finding the secret will help us rescue Galen from the far side of the moon."

"Plud?" said Eric. "The Forbidden City of Plud? The evilest of evil fortresses?"

"That's the place," said Neal.

The children looked at one another.

Max grunted softly. "So be it. We must go there if we hope to free my master."

"So be it, indeed," said King Zello. "But we must go different ways, my friends. We to Agrah-Voor and you to Plud. If what Kem says is true, I fear we must go as soon as we can —"

"Except the wingsnakes are still out there," said Khan, his nose twitching. "I can smell them."

Kem grumbled suddenly, and Neal laughed. "They won't be there for long. Kem has a trick."

The dog crept carefully to the entrance,

braced himself, then roared loudly — "*Grooo-oooo!*" The sound echoed throughout the cave as if it had come from a hundred beasts a hundred times Kem's size.

Eeeee! The wingsnakes shrieked in terror. Next came a wild flap of wings. The flapping and shrieking grew softer and softer until, in a few seconds, everything was quiet outside.

Zello poked his head out of the volcano entrance, then pulled it back in, laughing. "Nice work, Kem. Those snakes are long gone!"

The band of friends hurried out of hiding and stood together on the black land.

"I'll go with you, my king and queen," said Khan. "If there is trouble, I must protect my family and the rest of the Lumpies."

"A good king and a good man," said Zello, patting Khan on his tasseled shoulder.

"Keeah, take the Moon Medallion," said

Relna, removing the magical object from around her neck. "I'm sure you'll need this to find Galen. But remember, the darker the Dark Lands, the weaker our power."

"I'll remember," said Keeah, hugging both parents tightly. "You be safe, too!"

"Wait a second," said Neal. "Can anyone tell me how long the tangfruit's magic lasts?"

"Until you eat again," said Relna. "You must be careful not to eat as long as you wish to understand Kem."

Neal blinked. "Me? Not eat? Oh, this is going to be a *long* adventure!"

Finally, when there was no more to say, Zello, Relna, and Khan raced away across the Dark Lands toward the city of Agrah-Voor.

"We must get started, too!" said Max impatiently. "To the east. To the city of Plud!"

Kem yipped happily, then scampered over a rise in the land and down the other side, howling all the while. *"Ree-ooo-eeew!"*

"Well, you heard the dog," said Neal.

Julie grumbled. "We heard him, Neal, but we didn't exactly understand him."

Neal laughed. "Sorry. He's telling us we need to go now. It won't be long before those wingsnakes come back. With reinforcements. Follow that dog!"

And they did.

But as the kids raced into the east after Kem, the earth grew ever blacker, and the smoky air surrounded them like a cloud.

Three

O Plud, My Plud!

Not long after the friends left the volcano valley, the earth rose in a series of sharp hills. Steep passes wound narrowly between them.

"Careful, friends," said Max. "The Forbidden City of Plud is on the other side of these hills. There could be Ninns lurking nearby."

"Stay on guard," said Keeah, "and be alert."

As the little group trekked into the hills, they lost sight of the western lands entirely. The closer to Plud they pressed, the more they began to hear things. First, there was the sound of metal clashing on metal.

Cling! Clank! Clong!

Next came hissing — *ssss!* — and the distant squeaking of iron wheels — *errr! errr!*

"Whatever they're doing, the Ninns sound like they're up to no good," whispered Julie.

Half an hour later, the children emerged from the passes onto a ridge that overlooked a black plain. Beyond the gnarled and burned trees of a long-dead forest rose the terrible dark fortress of Plud. Its tallest tower was wrapped in the deep orange of endless flames, ever burning, ever coiling upward.

"The Forbidden City," said Eric, clasping his sword again. "Not a friendly place."

Kem whimpered quietly, and Neal nodded. "I know, boy. Plud is a *very* sad place —"

Just then, another sound broke on their ears. This time it was the jangle of armor and belt buckles. And it was coming from behind them.

"Get down!" said Julie, pulling her friends below an outcropping of rock on the ridge.

Thomp-thomp-thomp! A thudding band of armored red warriors rushed up the pass behind the kids. Reaching the end, their leader held up his hand, and the others stopped. He lifted a stubby finger to his lips and motioned to the left of the valley below. The Ninn troops nodded, drew their swords, and crept quietly down the hill to the fortress.

"What's going on?" whispered Keeah. "I counted a hundred Ninns there, armed for battle —"

"So then who's in Plud?" asked Max.

Creeping forward to the top of the ridge, they now saw who was in Plud.

Emerging all along the walls of the fortress was every kind of beast imaginable — scaled, winged, furred. Some looked like lions with spikes running down their backs. Others were giant wolves with extra-long claws. Still others were frightening combinations of serpents and bears, thickly hided, with thorny tails.

"Ko's beasts!" said Julie. "They've . . . they've taken over Plud. Just like they took over Sparr's volcano palace!"

"They've spotted those Ninns, too," said Eric. The beasts on the walls were clearly watching the little band of Ninns make their way toward the fortress. They wheeled a great ugly catapult to the very brink of the top tower and were aiming it carefully at the red warriors.

"They're going to ambush the Ninns," said Keeah. "It's not fair. We have to warn them!"

"I've got it," said Eric. Taking aim, he let loose a narrow silver beam from his fingertips. Sizzling through the air like a thread of light, it wound down to the head of the Ninn band, where it landed with a small *pop*.

The red warriors scattered in surprise just as the beasts fired their catapult. A large flaming rock exploded harmlessly in the path where the Ninns had just been.

"Excellent!" cried Max. "You saved them!"

"Uh, yeah," said Neal. "Except who's going to save us? Guys, we have company. . . ."

Before they could hide, the friends were surrounded by a second band of Ninns. Their leader pushed his face right into Eric's.

"You save Ninns with fingers!" the leader boomed. "Why? Why you *help* Ninns?"

Keeah gulped softly as she moved next to Eric, whose mouth was hanging wide open.

"Well, we didn't exactly *help*," she said. "We just didn't think the beasts were fighting fairly."

Eric nodded. "Uh-huh. What she said."

The Ninn straightened and looked down at Plud. He made a moaning sound that Eric thought might have been a sigh.

"Plud is . . . our home," he grunted. "One night, beasts come. They push us out. Now they use Plud to make weapons for Ko." He pointed to the plume of fire and smoke rising from the main tower. "Not good."

"Man," said Neal, "I never thought I'd think of Sparr's time as the good old days."

"Sparr," the Ninn murmured, that same moan in his voice. "Long time, no Sparr." He shook his head and looked down at the ground sadly.

"What's your name?" asked Keeah.

Slapping his six-fingered fist on his chest armor, the Ninn said, "Captain Bludge!"

"Captain Bludge," said Keeah, "Sparr told us that something in Plud will help us find our friend. He's up there . . . on the moon."

Bludge followed Keeah's gaze to the sky, then saw the Medallion around her neck. "There is door in Plud. Moon is above door."

"*Roooo!*" howled Kem.

"That must be where Sparr wants us to go!" said Julie. "Bludge, can you get us to this door? Can you show us this moon?"

The Ninn's face twisted into a strange expression. Eric wondered if it was a smile.

The warrior pointed his sword to the base of the fortress near the frozen lake. "We help you get in. You help us free Plud."

"Well, well," said Max, shaking his head. "We help the Ninns, and the Ninns help us? I suppose there's a first time for everything!"

In a flash, the Ninns assembled. Careful to remain hidden from the beasts, Bludge led the children, Max, and Kem down the side of the valley and around to the shore of the giant frozen lake. There they joined the first group of Ninns whom Eric's spark had warned.

"Princess of Droon," said Bludge. "You make . . . fog? Fog hide Ninns. We sneak in under beasts' noses. You sneak, too."

He pointed to a dark opening at the base of the fortress across the frozen lake, then made a gargling sound like laughter. "The sewer."

Neal frowned. "Excuse me? The sewer? The sewer of Plud? Do we have to?"

Keeah smiled. "I can make fog. Our friend on the moon taught me how."

With a quick wave of her hands and a brief whisper, she blew a breath out across the ice.

At once, a white mist rose up from the lake. It thickened and swirled until the kids could barely see the fortress in the distance.

Bludge chuckled softly. "Now, we slide!"

Together, Eric, Neal, Julie, Keeah, Max, Kem, and the Ninns slid unseen across the frozen lake.

Before long, they were on the opposite shore under the battlements. On Bludge's command, everyone pinched their noses and slipped one by one into the dark sewer opening. In no time, the band was through the sewers, up some stairs, and passing room after room filled with beasts forging swords and arrows.

"Ko make Plud worse," whispered Bludge, his eyes fixed on the black passage ahead.

Eric and Neal paused outside one chamber where some beasts were bowing before a figure all in black. "All hail messenger who speaks the words of Emperor Ko!" they said.

Then the dark figure spoke in a low voice.

"Beware tomorrow morning's fight!
Beware the flying silver light!
Beware a —"

"Who do you think that is?" asked Eric. "He's giving the beasts Ko's advice!"

"I don't know, but he rhymes," said Neal. "Plus, he sounds weirdly familiar —"

"You guys, come on. We found it!" whispered Julie, pulling the two boys down the hall to where everyone was crowded by a small door.

Carved over the door was a moon surrounded by a circle of stars. Eric recognized it as one of the marks on the Moon Medallion.

"We never go in here," said Bludge.

"Because you're afraid?" said Keeah.

"Because we too big to fit through door."

"Well, it's just my size," said Max. "Now behold something Galen taught *me*!" He fiddled with the lock. Then there was a soft *click*. Max grinned. "That makes two for the spider troll!"

"Good work, Max," said Neal.

Keeah turned to the Ninn leader. "Thanks, Bludge. Good luck in winning back Plud."

Bludge nodded once, then hurried away.

"And now we find what Sparr wants us to find," said Eric. Grabbing the knob, he leaned against the door and pushed.

The little door opened into a room that was dark except for a dull glow in the back corner. Squirming past everyone, Kem went straight for a small pile. He tugged out two objects shaped like birds. Holding them between his front paws, he began to bite them.

"Chew toys," said Neal, smiling. "Puppies are puppies no matter how many heads they have!"

Several old pieces of baby furniture were neatly stacked together, as if carefully preserved. But it was the light from the back that most drew their attention. Nearing it, they saw that it was actually a large black cloth, and the light was coming from under it.

"Well, what are we waiting for?" said Eric.

Taking hold of the cloth, the five friends gave a single, quick pull.

Whooosh!

The chamber blazed with sudden light.

"Ohh!" gasped Keeah, staggering back.

Once their eyes adjusted to the brightness, they all beheld a magnificent silver chariot hitched to a great, motionless silver horse. Both the horse and chariot had giant, sweeping wings.

"It's so beautiful!" gasped Max.

Eric glanced at the strange markings swimming across the chariot's silver surface. Without knowing how or why, he knew them as words and knew what they meant.

"It says, 'For my sons.' I think Zara made this chariot for Galen, Sparr, and Urik. I think this is what Sparr was talking about. This chariot will help us find Galen!"

On the chariot's railing, which started

in the front and ended in the rear, was a round blank place.

"What if the Medallion fits here?" said Keeah. Removing it from her neck, she inserted it into the railing. At once, the horse bristled as if it were alive. The chariot rocked on its wheels.

Suddenly, the small door burst open behind them. A bearlike beast yelled into the chamber. "Look! Children in Plud! And look! Silver for Ko's armor! Let's melt it!"

"No!" cried the voice of Bludge, who tore the beast away from the door. "Children, go!"

"Go?" cried Max. "But how?"

At the sound of thundering feet and yelling beasts, a tremendous clanking erupted from the back wall, as if a massive chain were being wound on to an iron wheel. Suddenly, the wall lifted to reveal a great spiral corridor, winding up inside the wall of the tower.

The silver horse quivered to life and began to pull the chariot to the open wall.

"*This* is how we go!" said Julie, scrambling into the moving chariot.

The instant everyone else piled in, the silver horse galloped into the black corridor and flew up inside the fortress tower, leaving the beasts and the Ninns far behind.

Four

Across a Clouded Room

"Ahhhh!" the kids and Max screamed as the silver horse charged up and around the pitch-black corridor to the top of the tower.

"What happens when we get to the top?" cried Julie.

"We'll probably fall," said Neal. "Again!"

Suddenly, the ceiling flew open and — *vooom!* — the chariot shot out into the light.

The beasts on the tower shrieked in

surprise and anger when the chariot blasted right past them and away from the fortress. Up it flew, mile after mile, leaving the ground far below.

"We're flying! We're flying!" said Julie. "We're going straight to the moon!"

"But who's driving this thing?" cried Neal.

"Eric, you found the Pearl Sea," said Keeah, pushing him in front. "You drive!"

The moment Eric put his hand on the Medallion and turned it — *whoooosh!* — the chariot soared straight through the black air of the Dark Lands and entered a gleaming sky of midnight blue, shimmering with stars and the big, bright face of the silver moon.

"So this is what it's like way up here, over the Dark Lands," said Eric. "It's awesome —"

"Hey, driver, pay attention!" cried Max,

pointing at a large cloud that was drifting toward them. "Watch out for that cloud!"

"No problem," said Eric. Though he didn't know why, he knew instinctively what to do. He turned the Medallion left, and the chariot veered left. "There —"

But the cloud suddenly went left, too.

When he steered the chariot right, the cloud went right. In fact, whichever way Eric drove, the cloud was there, closing in on them.

"Is that cloud *following* us?" said Neal.

Finally, the cloud surrounded them like a pair of hands trapping a lightning bug.

"Whoa, chariot!" said Eric, removing the Medallion. At once, the silver horse pulled the chariot to a stop on the floor of the cloud.

The little group sat waiting, surrounded by thick white air.

"Okay, this is weird," said Keeah.

"So now what?" said Neal.

"So now . . . *me!*" chuckled a pleasant voice.

A large red turban came floating out of the cloud toward them. Under it, dressed in colorful robes of green and white, waving at the mist with both hands, was a short, plump man with a wide grin on his face.

"Hoja?" said Eric, stepping out of the chariot and walking carefully across the cloud. "Hoja, the Seventh Genie of the Dove? Is that you?"

"Hoja, it is!" said the stout man.

"Yes!" said Keeah, jumping from the chariot and running to the short man.

The grin on the genie's face as he hugged the princess was nearly as large as the monstrous turban on his head.

"The last time we saw you was in the city of Ut," said Max. "You left us to follow Galen!"

"I *did* follow Galen," said Hoja, laughing under his turban. "But I couldn't save him alone. That's why I've been waiting for you!"

Neal frowned. "You were waiting for us? How did you know we would come here?"

"As you may recall from our time in Ut," said Hoja, motioning them to follow, "genies roam freely through time. I simply went from today to tomorrow and discovered that you would be coming here today, so I went back to yesterday and waited until tomorrow, which is today!"

Everyone stared at him.

Hoja shrugged. "Or something like that."

The cloud's floor was springy and made a soft warbling sound as the friends left the chariot and followed the genie. At the edge of the cloud, Hoja reached his hand into the mist, opened a misty door, and walked through into a second white room. In the center stood a table with dozens of maps and scrolls spread out on top.

"You see, my friends," said Hoja, "while Galen is not a genie himself, he has always had the love of one. Anusa, the beautiful Second Genie, took him on a journey to restore his youth."

"Would that be a . . . genie journey?" asked Neal with a laugh.

Hoja chuckled. "A journey of a thousand and one stops, actually. But as hard as I tried, I was never quite able to catch up with him."

"When the Pearl Sea showed us where Galen was, we saw black snow falling behind him," said Eric.

"Quite right," said Hoja, opening a scroll and pointing to a spot on it. "And the black snow flies right here in the city of Parthnoop!"

"Parthnoop?" said Max. "We've heard of that. It's where the flying urns come from!"

Hoja nodded. "Parthnoop is a place filled with wonders. It is — or was — a haven for many kinds of magical creatures from all over Droon, especially genies. But now Galen is in grave danger there. I might even say, all of Droon is in danger."

"Tell us what you know," said Keeah.

Hoja breathed deeply. "For ages, Parthnoop basked in the light of the sun, a glittering white city on the silver face of the moon. Until one day — or rather, one *night* — Fefforello, the Fifth Genie of the Dove, went a little — how shall I put this? — nutty, batty, loony, zany. As quickly as day turns to night, he turned to the dark side of his power. He wanted only to take control of everything!"

"So, the usual," said Julie.

"Exactly," said the genie. "Fefforello —

or the Sultan, as he calls himself now —
became a dark genie, turning Parthnoop
dark, too. He moved the entire city to the
far side of the moon, where the endless
black snow falls. And he trapped Galen in
his palace tower!"

The children were speechless.

"I agree!" said Hoja. "Perhaps even worse
is that the Sultan plans to attack Droon
from there. When I visited tomorrow, I
found out that unless we stop him today,
Droon will only be a yesterday."

Max grumbled angrily, "We must do
something! For Galen! And for Droon!"

"Zara's chariot can get to the far side
of the moon faster than anything," said
Neal. "Hoja, will you come with us?
Right now?"

The genie smiled an enormous smile.
"While it is wise to know the answer, it
is *truly* wise to know the question. The

answer to your question, Neal, is *yes, I will come*!"

In a sudden blur, Hoja gathered the scrolls and maps from the table and stuffed them into his cloak. Then he folded the table to the size of a cookie and popped it into his turban.

"Now *that* is awesome!" chirped Max.

"What a way to clean a room!" added Neal. "I wish I could do that."

"Oh, tsk, tsk!" said the genie, giggling. "Just a little thing genies can do. Now watch this!"

Hopping with the others into the waiting chariot, Hoja clapped his hands once, twice, three times, and the walls, ceilings, and floors of the cloud quivered, hooted, and flew apart — they became a fluttering flock of snow-white doves!

"That's amazing!" Julie gasped.

"I suppose," Hoja chuckled. "Let's go!"

Eric slipped the Medallion back into the chariot, and the silver horse soared like a giant bird straight on to the silver orb of the moon.

In no time, the chariot was sweeping above the moon's bright face, across craters, mountains, and the slithering remains of long-dry rivers to its dark side, where a storm of black flakes surrounded them instantly.

Keeping one eye on a scroll, the other on the ground below, Hoja pointed. "There it is!"

A giant city loomed below. While its buildings were white and fanciful, its towers whimsical and amusing, the darkness and the swirling black snow made it seem like a sad place.

"Parthnoop," said Hoja. "The home of the enchanted urns. And also home of the Sultan and his fearless urn men, imps who ride atop the flying urns looking for people to attack. They carry little whips and are always humming!"

"Sounds like fun," said Neal, petting Kem and raising his eyebrows.

Julie pointed to a tall white tower spiraling up from the city. "What's that?"

"The Sultan's palace, where Galen is trapped," said Hoja. "Come, be watchful of flying urns, and let's land. Quickly, now!"

Eric twisted the Medallion and the chariot descended into the streets of Parthnoop, surrounded by a whirlwind of ashen flakes.

Five

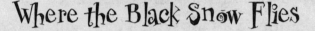

Where the Black Snow Flies

Eric drove the silver chariot into the stormy streets of Parthnoop, swooping low whenever anyone spotted a flying urn.

"Look there, a stable!" said Max, pointing through the flakes. "Perhaps we can hide the chariot there?"

"Good eye, Max," said Keeah. "Eric?"

"I see it." Eric dipped the chariot into an alley, landed gently, and drove up to a building with stone arches in front and a long row of stalls inside. Trotting into a stall, the silver horse stilled, as if asleep.

"Until we need you again," said Keeah, petting the horse. She and the others draped blankets over the chariot and horse until they were both completely hidden.

"And now . . . Parthnoop," said Hoja. He peeked out into the street. "Since the Sultan moved the city to the dark side, tourism has gone way down. That will make it more difficult to move through the streets unseen. But we must stay clear of the urn riders. Don't use your powers unless you have to, or we'll risk being seen and captured, just like Galen."

"Got it," said Keeah. "Use our brains, not our powers."

"Or our stomachs," murmured Neal. "Kem, no munching, or we won't understand each other." The puppy grumbled, but nodded both his heads.

Hoja led the children out of the stable and into the alley. "Our first order of business is to find Anusa. She remained free and has been trying to rescue Galen since his capture."

Darting to the end of the alley, the little band slipped down a narrow, snowy street and scrambled quickly to its end.

"Anusa is the Second Genie of the Dove," Julie said, turning to Hoja. "Fefforello is the Fifth. And you're the Seventh. So are you the youngest?"

"Oh, no. It doesn't work quite like that," said Hoja as they entered the cross street, careful to keep the tall palace tower in sight at all times. "As I told you, genies roam freely through time, so we haven't come about in any particular order. Of the seven of us, Anusa is called the second. The third and fourth are the twin babies, River and Stream. Fefforello is the fifth. And the sixth lives in the far east. She is a very old water genie named Jyme."

"But who's the first?" asked Neal.

Hoja paused at the end of the next street and looked out on a large white courtyard that was piled from end to end with black snow. The palace was on the far side.

"The First Genie?" said Hoja. "The last time I saw him was long ago, and he was very old. But he may not be so old now. Hard to tell."

The children looked silently at one another.

Hoja chuckled. "It is said that only he passed the ancient genie test of the Four Wonders in a single day. Not just that, but he performed a Fifth Wonder also!"

"What are the Wonders?" asked Max.

"I'm glad you asked," said Hoja. He cleared his throat and said, "To give to another, and yet receive. To follow another, and yet lead. To find another, and yet be found. And, perhaps the greatest of them all, to die for another, and yet live."

Neal nodded as he listened. Then he frowned. "A genie has to solve riddles, too."

"He does!" said Hoja. "In fact —"

"*Roooo!*" Kem yelped suddenly and raced into a side alley where a storm of black flakes whirled swiftly between the buildings.

"Hey!" said Neal, jumping after him. "Kem, get back here. We have to stay together —"

All at once — *whoosh! whoosh!* — there was a sound in the street behind them.

"Oh, no," said Max, spinning on his heels. "Is that what I think it is?"

In seconds, the street was filled with flying urns. On the urns sat dozens of impish creatures with turbans, flowing robes, shiny slippers, and tiny whips. The creatures were humming.

"Da-da-la-dum! Da-da-la-*dum*-dummm!"

"Urn riders!" hissed Hoja. "Hide!"

The urn riders raced up the alley just as everyone slipped around the corner. Everyone, that is, except Neal and Kem. They stood together, entranced by the whirling black flakes.

Whoosh! The urns zipped closer.

Neal! Eric called him silently with his powers, wanting to blast the riders but not daring to. *Get down!*

"They're going right for him!" hissed Julie.

All of a sudden, the black flakes swarmed over Neal and — *whoosh!* — the urn riders flashed by to the end of the alley, swerved around the corner, and disappeared without seeing either the boy or the dog.

Eric jumped to his feet. "I can't believe it!"

Just then, the snowstorm dissolved, and there in the street, not three paces away from Neal and Kem, stood a woman in white. A woman they had all seen before.

Keeah gasped. "Anusa!"

It was Anusa, the Second Genie of the Dove. She was dressed in flowing white robes, and she moved along the street toward them as if she were floating over the ground.

Her black hair glistened under a small white turban. It was braided with tiny bells that jangled softly when she moved.

Neal couldn't take his eyes off of her. "Uh, thanks, Anusa. I guess you saved me!"

Anusa smiled, speaking in a soft voice. "Because you saw me, the riders didn't see you."

"Anusa!" said Hoja, bowing to her.

"Hoja, it's good to see you," she said. "I've been expecting you all. Every attempt to free poor Galen has failed. But come, all of you. Time is passing quickly, even for us genies. Come."

While everyone followed, Anusa wove through the streets around the courtyard like a quick, gentle wind.

"The Sultan is clever," she told them. "I don't know what turned him suddenly evil, but clever and evil are a bad combination."

"Like it being lunchtime and not being able to eat," murmured Neal, scruffing Kem on the head.

"Indeed," said Anusa. "But unlike lunch, what the Sultan is planning is terrible — and it's going to happen soon."

"Which makes it even more important for us to get into the palace," said Julie.

"And look!" said Max, pointing to the

front of the palace. Four large urns were being rolled up to the gates by a dozen riders. They lifted a big black knocker on the gate, let it fall — *boom!* — and waited.

"It looks to me like urns are being delivered to the palace," the spider troll continued. Then he smiled. "Urns without passengers . . ."

Hoja nearly burst into laughter. "Well said, Max! With our little band of wizards, genies, a two-headed puppy, and a spider troll —"

"And me!" said Neal.

"And Neal," said Hoja, "we should be able to get into the palace in style — by urn!"

Helped by Anusa's whirling mass of black flakes, the little band of wizards, genies, a two-headed puppy, a spider troll, and Neal moved very close to the front steps.

Then, under the cover of a gust of snow, the kids hopped into the urns — Eric, Max, Neal, and Kem into one, Julie and Keeah in a second, and Anusa and Hoja in each of the last two.

When the gates finally opened — *errr!* — the urns were tipped on their sides — *thud!* — and the friends were rolled straight into the palace.

"Oh, my lunch!" groaned Neal as he dropped onto Eric, Max, and Kem.

"What lunch?" whispered Eric.

"The one I wish I was eating now instead of being rolled in an urn!" groaned Neal.

Thump! Thump! Thump! Thump! went the urns as the little men rolled them one by one into the Sultan's giant palace.

The Dark Genie

One moment Eric felt as if someone were dropping sandbags on him, and the next moment he felt as if he were the sandbag.

Thumpety-thumpety!

Finally, the rolling stopped.

"Heavy, these urns," squeaked one of the Sultan's urn men.

"Come on," said another. "Let's find out

if the Sultan wants them here or on the *Raven*."

"The *Raven*, right," laughed another. "Caw! Caw! Boom!"

Several sets of feet padded down the hall.

"Feel . . . sea . . . sick . . ." groaned Max.

"Wait," whispered Keeah. She and Julie popped their heads out of their urn and peeked around. "All right. It's clear."

"The *Raven*?" said Anusa, hopping out. "I don't like the sound of that. Let's find Galen and figure out what the Sultan is planning before it's too late."

Together the friends slipped down the hall and into a passage painted pink with purple polka dots and wavy yellow stripes.

"It's awfully colorful," whispered Julie.

"Yes, well, colorful or not," said Max, "I don't want any dark genie finding us here!"

Hoja paused. "Or will he find us, anyway?"

"What do you mean?" asked Keeah.

Anusa nodded. "I think Hoja means that because the Sultan is still a genie, he could have gone into the future to see what we'll do, and he could be waiting for us."

Eric looked down the next long hallway. "So you think we should do something totally unexpected?"

"I think," said Anusa, "that perhaps we should be . . . invisible!"

Hoja smiled from ear to ear. "Invisible? Oh, just the thing to fool a time-traveling genie."

Anusa pulled several tiny bottles from her turban, each containing what looked like a single drop of blue liquid.

"Swallow this, and you'll be invisible for as long as you need to be," said Anusa.

"Cough three times and you'll be visible again —"

"Too late!" squeaked a tiny voice suddenly. "The Sultan knew you would try to become invisible! So we arrived just before you did!"

Everyone turned to find the hallway filling with floating urns, each one crowded with a half-dozen turbaned riders.

"And now," squeaked the chief rider, "I believe you are our prisoners —"

"Not yet!" cried Anusa, flying up to the ceiling. "Children, run! Hoja, dive at the riders, scatter them!"

While the two genies swooped swiftly at the urn riders, the children raced down the hall as quickly as they could.

"Here!" said Anusa, tossing the kids a bottle of blue liquid. Before anyone could catch it, a rider snapped out with his little

whip, and the vial smashed on the floor —
crash!

"*Rooo!*" Kem ran over, licked up the blue
liquid, and — *plink!* — he vanished.

"Yay, Kem!" Julie yelled. "Run, boy, run!"

"Here's another!" said Anusa, tossing
a second bottle. Neal leaped high and
caught it.

By now a dozen more urns zoomed
into the hall. Half of them soared after Hoja
and Anusa, trapping them against the ceiling, while the other urns jetted after the
kids like little rockets. In a moment, they
surrounded Keeah, Max, and Julie. But Eric
and Neal blasted between two attackers and
kept running.

The two boys zigzagged through the
passages and all the way back to the front
gate before they realized their friends had
been captured. They finally stopped behind

the giant urns they had hidden inside to enter the palace.

"Oh, man!" said Eric breathlessly, peeking back down the hall. "They captured our friends! All of them! Now what'll we do?"

Neal looked out to see the riders sweep into the hall. He nudged Eric's shoulder and held out the blue bottle. "There's only one drop. Eric, you be invisible. I'll hide behind you."

Eric stared at his friend, then blinked. "Neal, if I'm invisible and you hide behind me, I'm pretty sure they'll see you."

As the riders floated closer and closer, Neal shook his head. "You're a wizard."

"I'll be an *invisible* wizard!" said Eric.

"I heard that!" snarled a sudden voice.

Suddenly, there he was, hovering cross-legged amid the approaching urn riders — the dark genie, the evil Sultan himself.

He was dressed all in black, from his

robes to his slippers. Instead of a gem, he wore a rough black stone in the center of his black turban. It was so dark that it seemed to draw light into it.

"Riders," he snarled, "the two wizards are hiding behind those urns. Watch as I trap them!"

"One wizard and a Neal," whispered Neal. "Take the potion, Eric. It'll save us both!"

"I don't think so, but okay!" said Eric. Just as he drank the potion, the Sultan zoomed up over the urns and hovered above them.

"What?" He looked behind the urns. He looked around the urns. He looked into the urns. He saw no one. "Where are they?" he bellowed.

"See?" said Neal, crouching behind his invisible friend. "He really *can't* see me!"

Eric sighed. "But he can *hear* you! Run!"

The two friends shot off down the hall and were around the corner in a flash.

"You won't get far!" boomed the angry Sultan, shaking his fists. "My tower is wizard-proof, so you'll never free Galen!"

"Dun-dun-dunnn!" chanted the riders.

"Not only that, but my secret, bird-shaped rocket, which I call the *Raven*, is nearly ready to attack Jaffa City! Soon you shall not just be invisible, you shall be no more!"

"Dun-dun-*dunnnnn!*" said the riders.

"But first, I shall go back in time and help the evil beasts win their war against Droon!"

"*DUNNNNNN!*"

Moments later — *whoosh!* — the Sultan and his men flew down the hall and were gone.

Eric and Neal stopped running and

stood side by side, trying to catch their breath.

"That Sultan is one crazy guy," said Eric.

"But at least the two of us are free," said Neal.

Eric frowned. "Two is a small team."

"Well, yeah," said Neal, stepping down the hall and peeking into a side passage. "But half of our team is an invisible wizard."

"You've got a point," said Eric, staring at his hand but not seeing it. "So let me get this straight. We need to find Galen —"

"That's first," said Neal, tapping a finger.

"Free all of our friends, and stop the Sultan from shooting off his weird rocket —"

"Which is shaped like a bird and called the *Raven*," said Neal. "That's two and three."

"Find invisible Kem," said Eric. "And finally drive Zara's chariot back to Droon."

Neal nodded, counting on his fingers. Then he frowned. "You forgot one."

"I don't think so," said Eric.

"You didn't say to duck," said Neal.

"Why should we duck?" asked Eric.

"Because a bunch of urn riders with whips are flying straight for us?" said Neal. "I think we should duck or we'll both have instant haircuts. Duck now. Eric — *duck now*!"

He pulled Eric to the floor as — *voooom!* — a troop of riders roared overhead, chanting the Sultan's name. "Feffo — Feffo — Feffo — rello!"

After they were gone, Eric stood and dusted himself off. "Not liking Parthnoop so much right now. Come on." He stepped past Neal and started down the hall.

"Right, except it's this way," said Neal, pointing to the side passage he had just noticed. "There are steps at the end of this hall. They probably lead up to the tower."

Eric sighed. "I'm glad someone's paying attention around here. Come on!"

Afraid for his friends but hoping he would soon find Galen, Eric led the way into the narrow passage and up the stairs, with Neal following swiftly behind him.

Seven

As the Doorknob Turns

When Eric and Neal were halfway up the tower stairs, they realized that the stairs curved around in an ever tighter spiral, and the ceiling lowered with each step closer to the top.

"It's getting a little cramped here," said Eric, bumping his head and scraping his shoulders against the stones. "I'll have to crawl."

Neal looked up at where Eric's voice

was coming from. "I can't tell you how weird it is to be talking to an empty space."

"I wish I *were* an empty space," said Eric. "Then maybe I could fit in here!"

When they had finally inched up the last few steps on their stomachs, they stopped. At the top of the stairs stood a solid wall.

Eric blinked. "What is this, a joke? I'm going to blast it —"

"Eric, don't," said Neal. "Crazy Feffy said the tower is wizard-proof."

"We'll see about that!" Eric aimed up at the wall and shot a single blast at it. *Blammm!* It bounced off the wall, ricocheted off the ceiling, and exploded over the boys' heads, nearly frying them.

Neal groaned. "Well, that didn't work."

"Sorry," said Eric. "I thought *nothing* was wizard-proof."

"If it wasn't wizard-proof, would Galen

have stayed locked up in there for so long?"

Eric made a face. "You with the questions. Maybe we should just go back down —"

"Except that when you blasted the wall, I think I saw something. Let me try. . . ." Neal reached up and moved his hand over the wall. Then he chuckled. "Ah, yes. The door."

"The door?" said Eric, annoyed. "Cut it out. There is no door. That's the whole problem."

"Oh, yeah?" said Neal. He turned his hand with a slight twist. There was a soft *click, a squeak — errrr!* — and a door-shaped opening appeared on the wall. "Ta-da!"

Eric gasped. "How did you do that?"

"Doorknobs turn," said Neal.

Eric shook his head. "No, really, how did you —"

"Maybe it's the tangfruit helping me. You should eat more fruit, Eric. It's good for you."

"Uh-huh," said Eric, squirming up in front of the door. "Or maybe it's because this tower is wizard-proof, and I'm a wizard?"

Neal looked thoughtful. "So we're saying that sometimes it's good *not* to be a wizard?"

Eric shrugged, pulled open the door, and walked into a room blazing with light. Neal followed closely behind his invisible friend.

"Neal!" said a voice. "You found me!"

There, in the middle of a small room, stood a tall man in a blue robe.

The man was Galen.

Or rather, it was Galen as he might have looked a hundred years earlier.

The wizard was younger. His face was

hearty and smiling. He seemed taller. His beard, while still white, was shorter, as was his hair. He wore his familiar wizard cloak and hat, but they looked new, as if they had just come from the cleaners. Around his waist was a short, curved staff, softly shimmering in green, then in blue, then red, then silver.

He grinned. "Neal! After all this time, it was you! I'm so happy to see you —"

"Hey, I'm here, too!" said Eric.

Galen blinked. "Eric? I can't see you."

"Oh, sorry." Eric coughed three times, and — *plink!* — he was visible again.

"My wonderful friends!" boomed Galen, hugging them both. "It's been far too long —" Just then, Galen saw the sword at Eric's side and gasped. "My mother made that sword!"

"That's just the beginning!" said Neal.

The two boys told Galen as quickly as they could everything that had happened since they last saw him — how Sparr had become a boy, how Ko and Gethwing emerged as new villains, how the magic staircase had vanished and how they had helped to restore it, how Eric had found the Pearl Sea and Zara's sword — until Galen finally had to tell them to stop.

"Boys, boys, too much information! There's a time and a place for all of those tales of the past. And I do want to hear them, in fact I'm quite anxious to hear them, but right now we must leave this place. The Sultan is up to something large and terrible. Tell me what you know!"

As they made their way down the stairs, the boys told Galen as much as they knew about the rocket called the *Raven* that was set to attack Jaffa City. They also told him how Keeah, Julie, Max, Hoja, and Anusa had been captured by the Sultan's evil urn riders.

"Anusa," said Galen, smiling, when they stepped from the stairs and into the passage. "It was her love that saved me. I only hope that now mine can save her. Friends, this isn't good. Not at all. We must get that black stone out of Fefforello's turban. It is that stone that turned him to the dark side."

"What is the stone all about?" asked Eric. "It looks like a regular old rock to me."

His eyes darting both ways, Galen crept down the passage to the main hall. "Every genie journey ends by finding something of great value. My quest took me to this stone. At once, I knew it had great power, for either good or evil. I also knew that it was not meant for me, but for someone else."

"For who?" asked Eric.

The wizard turned to him. "That, my friend, is a question I hope my books and scrolls will answer. Before consulting the old legends, however, this stone must remain a mystery. But what happened to Fefforello is not a mystery. Once Anusa brought me here to Parthnoop to rest after my journey, Fefforello saw the stone and — zoop! — he was conquered by its raw power."

"How will we get it back?" asked Neal. "Fight him and force him to give it to us?"

"Force him?" said Galen, pausing at a corner where two passages crossed. "I don't think so. Trick him, perhaps. I like that better. But know this, his little urn men are really his doves under an evil charm. When we have the stone again, Fefforello will be free, but he may not remember the charm to turn his riders back into doves. So they will still be against us —"

Galen stopped short, his staff sizzling in the hallway's dim light. "And here they are."

And there they were, a dozen urns flying around the corner, each with six little urn riders perched on top. The urns lined up and parted. Then the Sultan floated between them, carrying a long sword.

"Sssso, Galen!" the Sultan said, snarling like a snake. "Your little friends helped you escape my wizard-proof tower? Should we battle now? Urn riders, watch and learn!"

"Dun-dunnnn!" the riders chanted.

Eric drew his sword and stepped forward. Neal huddled behind him.

"Wait for my signal, boys," Galen whispered over his shoulder, "then run for the stone. And remember, the urn riders are good creatures under a bad spell. No hurting them —"

"Enough mumbling!" shouted the Sultan.

He jumped toward Galen with his sword straight out in front of him. The wizard leaped aside and swung his colored staff with incredible speed, cutting intricate designs in the air.

Fwish-fwish-fwish! Each time the Sultan could have struck Galen, the wizard whirled his staff like lightning, causing the genie to twirl dizzily on his heels. Again and again he did this until, finally, the Sultan tumbled into the hovering urn riders, gasping for breath. "Wait . . . stop . . . can't breathe . . ."

When the dark genie pulled off his turban to wipe his brow, Galen yelled, "Boys, now!"

At once, Eric and Neal leaped out from behind the wizard, snatched the Sultan's turban, and yanked the black stone from it.

There was a flash of light in the hall. The Sultan screamed, "Ohhhh!"

Suddenly, the black of his genie robes

seemed to drain away, leaving him standing in an outfit of sparkling blue with pale yellow stripes.

Fefforello dropped his sword to the ground with a clang, then jumped back from it, surprised. "Oh! A sword? Please tell me I was slicing bread! Have I been bad or something?"

"Let's just say *or something*," Galen answered. "But no, Fefforello, you could never be *bad*!"

"Well, *we're* bad!" cried one of the urn men. "We're still evil! And we'll still get you!"

"What did I tell you?" said Galen, pulling Eric and Neal away from the advancing riders. "Fefforello, we'll deal with the riders. You try to free our friends and your fellow genies."

"I will!" said Fefforello. *Pooof!* In a flash of light and smoke, he was gone.

"Now," said Galen, leaping down the hall, "let's use the smoke to escape. Climb out the window and onto the roof, boys. Our adventure's not over!"

"I love the sound of that!" said Eric, clambering through the window.

The three friends tore across the roof, jumped down to the next roof, then climbed up a balcony to a third one. From one roof to another they raced, putting more distance between themselves and the main palace.

All of a sudden, they heard the sound of feet pattering across the roof tiles in front of them.

"Careful," said Eric, slowing.

There was a tiny cough. Then another, and finally a third. *Plink!* Kem was standing on the edge of the roof, wagging his tail. Both of his tongues were hanging out.

"*Roo-eee-rrrooww!*" he wailed.

"Kem!" said Neal, running to him and scooping him up in his arms as the puppy continued to howl. "Wait. What? Guys, Kem says he found the biggest chew toy ever. It's shaped like a big black bird."

"*Rooo!*" wailed the puppy.

"The *Raven!*" said Galen. "Take us to that rocket, little Kem. We shall follow you!"

"And we'll follow *you!*" yelled a familiar voice as Keeah climbed over a neighboring rooftop, followed by Julie and Max. She smiled widely when she saw Galen. "Fefforello just freed us —"

"Master!" cried Max. He leaped across the air to Galen, and the two hugged.

But the reunion didn't last long.

"There they are!" snarled the chief urn man, finally tumbling out the smoky window in front of a troop of flying riders. "Get them!"

"Oh, man!" said Eric. *"Run!"*

As the six friends and Kem tore across the rooftops of Parthnoop, the turbaned riders swooped after them, their chants growing louder and louder.

"Dun-dun. Dun-dun! DUN-DUNNNN!"

Eight

A Roof with a View

"*Dun*-dun-*dun*-dun!" sang the urn men as they dived at the friends.

"Nice to have a soundtrack," Julie called over her shoulder as she ran. "It makes me feel like moving — fast!"

Suddenly, Kem skittered to the edge of one roof and stopped. His right head was pointing one way while his left head looked in the opposite direction.

"Everybody, look what Kem found!" said Neal, screeching to a halt.

In one direction was a monstrous black rocket, complete with wings and a massive beak, rising up from the ground in the distance.

"The *Raven!*" murmured Keeah.

Kem's other head pointed across the street to a small alley. At the end of the alley stood a stable with stone arches in front.

"That's where the chariot is!" said Julie.

Galen peered over the edge of the roof. "Ten feet," he whispered. "I wonder. I hate to be rude to the urn men but, shall we?" The kids nodded.

"Shall you *what*?" asked the chief rider, zooming over with his entire troop.

"Too-da-loo!" shouted Max, clutching Galen's hand. And before the urn men could stop them, the seven friends leaped

off the edge of the roof and hit the ground running.

"After them!" yelled the riders, swooping down into the street.

Racing along the alley, the friends charged into the stable. While Eric, Neal, and Max bolted the doors behind them, Galen went to the back of the stable and, holding his breath, pulled away the cloth hiding the chariot.

"Ahhhh . . ." he gasped, staggering in the glow of his mother's creation. "I *do* remember this!" He patted the head of the silver horse and ran his fingers over the carved symbols. "I can't believe Sparr kept it all these years."

"Master?" said Max.

The wizard turned to his friend. "I know. Time to ride!" He hopped into the chariot.

"All aboard?" asked Keeah.

"All aboard!" said Julie, making room for Neal and Kem beside her.

"Let's fly!" said Eric. The moment he slipped the Moon Medallion into its place on the chariot's railing, the silver horse sprang to life. In a flash, Queen Zara's chariot burst right through the stable doors, toppling the surprised urn men. It swept through the alley and finally soared up over the streets.

But the urn men raised an alarm instantly. Swooping bands of colorful urns came flying from every part of the snow-swept city.

"Up!" said Eric, moving the Moon Medallion, and the chariot flew up in a wide loop over the heads of the approaching riders. It zoomed between two slanted towers.

"They're gaining on us!" cried Max.

"Faster!" said Galen, his eyes fixed in front of them.

"More urns ahead!" Keeah called out. "Eric, drive us low. Dip the chariot!"

"I'm dipping!" he answered, twisting the Medallion. The chariot swooped below the oncoming urns and into the street.

Swoosh! Swoosh! No sooner had the chariot swept down than the urns, in a hurricane of swirling black flakes, dived after it.

When the chariot zoomed up once again, the friends saw the great bird-shaped vessel called the *Raven* looming straight ahead of them. The rocket was sleeker and blacker and more terrifying than any of them had realized. As it stood perched and ready to lift off, another troop of urn men filed inside a giant hatch on the rocket's tail.

"Brrrr-ump-bump!" sang the little men.

"Oh, my gosh!" said Keeah. "They're flying that . . . *thing* . . . to Jaffa City?"

"Not if we can help it!" cried several voices together.

All of a sudden, three figures flew down from the swirling, black-flaked sky — Anusa, Hoja, and Fefforello.

"My friends helped me remember the charm I put on my doves!" said Fefforello, resplendent in his blue robes and sparkling slippers. "Be gone, you impish men with bad attitudes. Return, my beautiful white doves!"

Then, whispering all together, and ending with three loud claps — *Clap! Clap! Clap!* — the genies reversed Fefforello's evil charm. As everyone watched, the riders quivered and yelped and finally turned into a cooing, fluttering flock of pure-white doves once more.

"Amazing!" chirped Max.

"I remembered more!" said Fefforello.

With a second round of claps, the genies whispered again, and the *Raven* collapsed into a swirl of black snow and vanished.

"Finally, this is the best part," said Fefforello. Clapping three more times, the Fifth Genie of the Dove twirled in his slippers. As he did, the city around them began to wobble. It quivered. It wiggled. Then finally it moved, lifting up from the surface and flying all the way from the moon's dark side into its blazing sunlight. If anyone thought Parthnoop was beautiful before, it was nothing compared to the awesome city that sparkled before them now.

"Ta-da!" said Fefforello.

"A new Parthnoop!" Galen boomed happily. "The ancient city of genies is restored!"

Whatever black snow there was, melted away in the heat and light. The swirling dark flakes were nowhere to be seen.

For a moment.

As everyone stood and gazed upon the great white city, Eric saw one tiny dark flake fall through the air. He caught it in the palm of his hand, but it didn't dissolve.

"Wait. This isn't snow," he said as more flakes began to fall all around them.

"No, not snow," said Max. "It's ash. Look."

Turning, they saw a thin stream of black ash in the sky, leading all the way back from Parthnoop to Sparr's Forbidden City of Plud.

"Plud's tower is flaming higher and higher," said Keeah. "The beasts and the Ninns must be fighting."

"Guys, I think our adventure might not be over," said Neal. "We have to go back to Droon. To Plud. And we have to go now."

Anusa turned to Galen. "Go. We shall meet you in Plud soon," she said. "There is something we genies must do first." Then, with a twirl of their colorful robes, all three genies vanished.

The wizard nodded. "Well then, friends, it is time. Shall we go to Plud?"

"To Plud!" said Eric.

In no time, the silver chariot whisked them up from the ground, and away they flew from the sparkling white city of Parthnoop to the dismal, dark, fearful city of Plud.

Nine

You Call This a Battle?

Swoosh! The chariot wound down through the smoky air of the Dark Lands and circled behind the Ninn encampment.

"I see things are changing in Droon," said Galen as they landed. "We have new friends to help us fight against the beasts now. This is good!"

Captain Bludge hustled right over to them. He and the wizard bowed to each other. "It got worse," Bludge said, pointing to the fortress. "More beasts come. Look."

More gray beasts than they could have imagined were ranged across Plud's walls. Every inch of the fortress was alive with them. Their red eyes gleamed in the light of many flaming torches.

The chief of the Ninns groaned and turned away from his former home. "Our Plud —"

"Will be yours again," said Galen firmly, "if we have anything to say about it."

The red warrior looked at the wizard. "You are Galen. For long time we are enemies."

Galen shook his head. "Not today, my friend. But we'll discuss all that later. For now, turning back the beasts is turning back Ko. And Ko must go!"

"But how will we get into the fortress?" asked Julie. "I've never seen so many beasts."

Captain Bludge looked thoughtful. "We attack front gate," he grunted. "You attack there." He pointed a stubby finger far to the east. Near where the walls of the fortress met the cliffs was a small, round pipe.

Bludge continued, "Beasts not ready for attack there. That is kitchen pipe."

"Kitchen?" said Neal, perking up at the word. "Do you think the beasts eat lunch?"

"Neal!" snapped Julie. "You can't eat until we're done here. Kem, either!"

Neal gave the dog a pat on each head. "Life is tough, isn't it, boy?" he grumbled.

"*Rrrr!*" Kem agreed.

"Bludge, that is an excellent plan," said Galen. "We'll enter Plud and battle the beasts from inside."

While the Ninns massed in a single army to charge the heavily guarded front gate, the kids, Max, and Kem, under Galen's stealthy lead, rode the chariot carefully through the surrounding forest until they were close under the high cliffs. There, they waited among the black trees for the red warriors to begin the attack. They didn't have to wait long.

"To Plud!" came the battle cry of the Ninns as they charged across the plain to the fortress's front gate.

"To Plud!" repeated Galen. "Eric, fly us straight inside the fortress!"

Except that he couldn't. The instant Eric drove the chariot near the fortress, the kitchen pipe echoed with a high shriek — *eeeee!* — and ten wingsnakes swooped right out at them.

"Eric, get us out of here!" cried Keeah. "The beasts must have expected us!"

"That way!" said Julie, pointing to the unmanned upper walls of the fortress.

Eric turned the Medallion and flew the

chariot unseen through the smoke, only to find a second band of wingsnakes swooping over the high walls at them there.

Four more attempts to surprise the beasts led to four more failures. Meanwhile, the Ninns were forced back across the plains.

"They know exactly what we're going to do!" grumbled Eric, finally driving the chariot back to the forest as the battle came to a pause.

"How could the beasts know?" asked Keeah. "It's like someone's telling them —"

Neal gasped suddenly. "No. Not *telling* them. *Told* them! Fefforello! Eric, don't you remember? Back when he was the bad Sultan, Fefforello said he would help Ko. This must be what he meant. He's a genie, so he must have gone ahead in time to see what we would do. Then he went back in time and told the beasts."

"You mean the Sultan was that shadowy figure we saw in Plud?" asked Eric.

"I'm pretty sure," said Neal.

"If only the genies were with us now," said Galen, pacing back and forth in front of the chariot. "It might be our only chance —"

"Too late!" cried Julie. "Catapult!"

Blammm! A fireball exploded nearby, sending everyone for cover in the chariot. As a second fireball zoomed toward them, Eric spun the Medallion and drove the silver vehicle back over the dark trees. He zigzagged across the sky until they were safely back in the Ninn camp.

Captain Bludge, his sword at his side, hurried over to them. "Plud is lost. The beasts have won." Suddenly, he paused. "Wait," he said. "Where is other boy?"

Galen whirled around on his heels. His

eyes widened. "Neal. Neal! Where's Neal? We couldn't have left him in the forest!"

"Not in the forest! There!" said Max.

Everyone turned to see the tiny figure of a boy with blond hair chasing a two-headed dog across the open ground beneath the walls. Five wingsnakes were closing in on him, their fiery breath nipping at his heels.

"Neal!" cried Eric, feeling his knees go weak. The wingsnakes drove Kem and Neal toward the lake. A moment later, Eric heard the ice crack and the water splash. The two figures vanished under the surface of the lake. "No! No! Neal —"

"Yeah, what?" said a familiar voice.

Everyone turned to see Neal standing behind them. He was soaking wet but smiling, and he had a wet Kem wrapped in his arms. "Hey, guys."

Keeah gasped. "Neal, you were just

down there! But now you're here. How . . . how . . ."

Neal held up his hand. "Hold on . . . five . . . four . . . three . . . watch this . . ."

He pointed to Plud.

All of a sudden, a wild shriek echoed from the main tower and across the plains, getting louder by the second. The next moment, the main gates burst open and the beasts — every last one of them — rushed away from Plud.

They leaped, they flew, they crawled, they ran. From the walls and the towers, from the halls and the sewers, from the dungeons and weapon rooms, the army of Ko's beasts fled the giant fortress of Plud.

It was over in a matter of minutes.

Before there were any more blasts, before an arrow was fired, before a single Ninn or beast yelled, "Ouch!" the vast legion of beasts had run away, far away, into the deepest, darkest distance of the Dark Lands.

The Forbidden City of Plud was empty.

"Pretty cool, huh?" said Neal.

"*Rooo!*" Kem agreed.

Ten

The Neal Factor

Eric practically jumped in the air. "What? No. Wait. This is impossible! Neal, how did you get here? We just saw you down there! Why did the beasts run away? Where have you been?"

Neal shrugged. "I think it's more *when* I've been. And I think the answer is yesterday."

"Yesterday?" said Max.

Galen peered closely at the boy. "Neal?"

"No, really. It was weird," said Neal. "When that big fireball struck near us in the forest, Kem got spooked and tore off. I raced after him and you guys left. Then a bunch of wingsnakes shot after me. They were a half second from frying me when I finally caught up to Kem at the lake. We cracked through the ice. I fell like a stone. Then, it was like — pooof! — and there I was, in that sewer from yesterday."

"Yesterday," repeated Max.

Neal nodded. "I knew it was yesterday because I saw *us* sneaking up the sewer behind me. At first I thought, *Huh? Did that tangfruit do something crazy to me?* But then I was pretty sure I must have gone back in time and that maybe that weird shadowy guy with the beasts wasn't the Sultan at all. Maybe it was me! So I covered myself in the chariot's black cloth and pretended to be a friend of Ko's and told the beasts a prophecy. Then I hid the chariot under the cloth again and — pooof! — here I am!"

Everyone was staring at him, their eyes huge and their mouths hanging open.

"You want to hear what I told the beasts?" Neal coughed, then grinned, then said in an eerie voice:

> *"Beware tomorrow morning's fight!*
> *Beware the flying silver light!*
> *Beware a boy so blond and cute,*
> *For when you see him, you must scoot!"*

As they all kept staring at him, there came the sound of fluttering in the air. A moment later, Anusa, Hoja, and Fefforello materialized and hovered above them. With them were three others, a pair of tiny twins and an old woman — River, Stream, and Jyme.

"All six genies!" said Galen, bowing.

Anusa, Hoja, and Fefforello looked at one another, their eyes huge and brimming with joy. "All seven genies, you mean," said Hoja.

With expressions full of astonishment and excitement, the six genies turned to Neal and bowed low before him until their turbans touched the ground.

Then they spoke in a single voice. "All hail the First Genie of the Dove!"

Neal began to wobble. "Uh . . . what? Who? No, this isn't right." He turned completely around. "Somebody had better cough three times, or else it looks like you're talking to me!"

"We are!" said Fefforello. "And it's true. We honor you, Neal Kroger, Genie of Genies!"

"A little birdie told us," said Anusa. "In fact, a million birdies told us." As she said this, the sky was alive with snow-white doves, fluttering together like a giant warbling cloud.

Neal finally slumped down to the ground, stammering, "But . . . but . . . but . . . but . . ."

"You accomplished the Four Genie Wonders, Neal," said Hoja.

He looked up. "I did?"

The genie nodded. "You gave Eric the potion, yet you received invisibility when you needed it; you told him how to find the tower, yet you followed him up the stairs; you found Galen where others had failed, and yet you found yourself as a genie. And just now, you risked your life to save a friend — you 'died' underwater — yet here you are! Neal, you are a genie. You finally have powers."

For a long time, everyone just looked at Neal, who had begun counting on his fingers. They were waiting for him to speak.

Finally, he did. "Okay. But one question. If I really am a genie, do I get a cool name, too?"

Everyone laughed.

"You do!" said Hoja. "For instance, my name was not always Hoja. Oh, no. I was born with the name Bobba-bobba-bobba-batta!"

The children stared at him.

"Your name is . . . Bob?" said Julie.

He winked. "You see why I chose Hoja?"

Neal thought for a second, but only for a second. "Then I want to be Zabilac, First Genie of the Dove!"

"It's beautiful," said Anusa.

"And it sounds familiar," said Keeah.

Neal grinned. "It's Calibaz spelled backward," he said.

"As for powers," said the genie named Jyme, "this will tell you everything you need to know."

Poof! A long golden-tipped scroll appeared out of nowhere. Floating next to it was an enormous blue turban speckled with white, silver, and green gems.

"The First Genie commands doves like no other," said Fefforello, setting the turban on Neal's head. "Normal genies have a hundred doves, but you command a hundred million! As you know, they can assume any shape."

Neal looked up at the glimmering surface of the moon. "How about . . . a road? Can the doves make a road?"

The genies looked at one another.

"Certainly," said Anusa. "But why?"

"I think I know," said Eric. He looked into the distant sky over the volcano palace. It was the place where their adventure had begun. "A road from Calibaz to Parthnoop? So the hoobahs can finally have a home?"

Neal smiled. "Yeah. They've been waiting for a long time."

"No sooner wished than done," said Anusa. "Zabilac, behold your doves!"

At once, the birds that had been fluttering around them flew high up over the volcano palace and wove a feathery road from the pit of Calibaz to the silver surface of the moon.

Neal pulled the hoobah horn out of his pocket and blew into it. Its melody soared into the sky. Before long, the small froglike creatures emerged from Calibaz. They wound down the road, one and all, as if

they had been waiting for the sound of Neal's horn.

"Just like the legend," said Eric. "A hero was destined to free the hoobahs from their dark life and lead them into the light. That hero is *you*, Neal."

"And that is the Fifth Wonder!" said Hoja, bowing again with everyone else.

While Neal kept playing the horn, the hoobahs, some on foot, some riding giant, blue, shovel-nosed beasts, made their way across the winding ribbon of fluttering doves all the way up to the silvery streets of Parthnoop, beaming in the light of Droon's sun.

"My boy," said Galen, "you've done a wonderful thing today."

Anusa smiled. "The first of many, I think."

"By the way," said Fefforello, "our very

first genie convention will be seven hundred years ago. Can you make it?"

Neal grinned. "Will there be lunch?"

"There were a hundred lunches!" said Hoja.

Neal laughed. "I think I'm already there!"

At that, the twin baby genies began to giggle.

"Now, we must go and set an extra place for lunch!" said Jyme. "See you a long time ago, Zabilac!"

Then all six genies began to vanish, though Anusa more slowly than the others.

"Anusa, my dove," said Galen, "your love made me young again."

"There is much I must do now," she said, not taking her eyes off the wizard.

He smiled. "I know. And there is much for me, too. But now that we have found each other again, we are only a whisper away."

Anusa laughed brightly as she disappeared, sharing Galen's gaze until the last moment.

The wizard laughed softly. "Oh, yes," he murmured, "the adventure shall continue!"

Ten minutes later, the chariot swept into the main gates of Plud. Eric moved the Medallion and steered the horse through the passages until at last they reached Sparr's main hall.

"It won't ever be hidden again," said Galen, running his hands over the silver rails one last time. "If my mother built it for her sons, perhaps we shall need it to save Sparr. And perhaps, someday, even to find my brother Urik, wherever in time or place he may be. Ninns, guard this well. It may yet play a role in Droon's future. Until then, keep it safe."

Together, Bludge and his army of warriors stood at attention before the silver chariot.

"And who knows," said Eric, taking Zara's sword from his belt. "Maybe Sparr will need this, too. I didn't even use it once today." He set it next to the chariot.

Keeah removed the Moon Medallion from the chariot and hung it around her neck again.

With a silent nod to the Ninns, the children, Max, Kem, and Galen left the fortress.

"Plud doesn't seem so forbidden anymore, does it?" asked Keeah.

Julie smiled as the giant gates closed softly. "No. Not so much."

"Perhaps we have begun to bring light to the darkness," said Galen. From his robe, he pulled out the dark stone. "Who knows? In this lump may lie the very future of

Droon. And, perhaps, of everything else, too."

They all stood in silent awe of the stone.

Finally, Neal spoke. "It reminds me of a coal from my barbecue grill."

Julie laughed. "Trust Neal to put things in perspective!"

"And speaking of food," said Neal, stooping to Kem. "Boy, I'm going home to eat. But maybe there will be a next time for us?"

"*Rooo!*" affirmed Kem.

Just then — *whoosh!* — the magical staircase appeared, gleaming in the sky above the black plains of Plud.

"We have to go home now," said Eric.

"And we have to find my parents in Agrah-Voor," said Keeah. "Ko is up to something evil. I only hope that Sparr is still safe."

"A new mystery calls us to a new adventure," said Galen, drawing his staff from his belt and setting his sights on the distant south. "How good it feels to be back in the game!"

"Just like old times," said Max as he wiped away a tear of joy.

"And just like new times!" said Neal, folding his turban and scroll to the size of cookies and slipping them into his pocket.

"We'll be back," said Eric. "Soon, I think."

"Soon, I *know!*" said Keeah with a laugh. Then, waving good-bye, she, Max, Kem, and Galen set out together across the plains.

Neal grinned at his friends. "Race you up the stairs?"

"You're on!" said Julie.

"Let's go!" said Eric. "Last one up is —"

But before he could move, Neal and Julie flew straight past him — *whoosh!* — and were already on the top step looking down.

Eric shrugged and laughed. "The last one up . . . is me!"

Then, as quickly as he could, Eric ran up to his friends and back to his normal life once more.